Advance praise for *The Whisper in the Ruins*

"Lisa Hendey's original take on the very popular St. Francis of Assisi emphasizes his deep desire to find out God's will for him and to live a life of mercy toward others. Young Chime Travelers readers, like Patrick, will be inspired to do the same!"
—BARB SZYSZKIEWICZ, OFS, editor and blogger, FranciscanMom.com

"The Chime Travelers books are worth putting on your 'buy for every kid you love' list. These adventures will make you think, teach you both history and faith, and inspire smiles and chuckles. You won't want to put them down!"
—SARAH REINHARD, Catholic blogger, author, *Word by Word*

"Lisa Hendey loves her faith, and that love shines through. Young readers will be entertained without realizing they're also learning a little more what it means to be a Catholic."
—RACHEL BALDUCCI, author, *How Do You Tuck In a Superhero* and cohost, *The Gist*

"After reading *The Secret of the Shamrock* our second-grade class invited Lisa Hendey for an 'author visit.' She kept the students engaged, grew their understanding of the beauty of our Catholic faith, and shared the joy of writing. Now the students can't wait to read the next book in her Chime Travelers series."
—WENDY REVELL, Our Lady of Perpetual Help School, Clovis, CA

"Lisa Hendey's Chime Travelers series delivers Catholic values in an entertaining fashion that will delight the young and young at heart. This father of five can't wait for the next volume."
—PETE SOCKS, The Catholic Book Blogger

**franciscan**
media
Cincinnati, Ohio

# The Whisper in the Ruins

LISA M. HENDEY

ILLUSTRATED BY JENN BOWER

Note: This work of fiction is inspired by events from the life of St. Francis of Assisi. Certain events are portrayed out of chronological order to facilitate the telling of this story.

Cover and book design by Mark Sullivan
All illustrations by Jenn Bower

Library of Congress Control Number
ISBN 978-1-63253-036-3

Published by Franciscan Media
28 W. Liberty St.
Cincinnati, OH 45202
www.FranciscanMedia.org

Printed in the United States of America.
Printed on acid-free paper.
19 20 21 22 23  8 7 6 5 4

# ▲ Chapter One ▲

Grrr...

Ribbit... ribbit...

Grrr...

*Bbrriiinnngggg!*

As the morning bell called the students to the start of the school day on a crisp October morning, one very brave tree frog glared up at a bulldog who was ten times his size.

"Calm down, Francis," Patrick soothed his fist-sized green pet. "Peter, can't you get Leo under control?"

"Cool it, Leo," Peter mumbled to his bulldog, without looking up at the frog's redheaded owner.

"Let's go, guys!" shouted Katie, Patrick's twin sister. "The Pet Blessing is starting!"

The Pet Blessing was an annual tradition at St. Anne's School on the feast day of St. Francis. The pastor, Father Miguel, stood at one end of the pavement next to Mr. Sarkisian and the choir. He was trying to get the attention of several hundred students and their furry friends. Nearby, the twins' teacher, Mr. Birks, did his best to round up his class and their animals.

"What was up with Peter?" Katie whispered to her brother, her green eyes catching his.

"Why was he in such a bad mood?"

"Who knows?" Patrick shrugged. "But with Leo looking like he wanted to eat Francis for lunch, I wasn't gonna stick around to find out!"

Katie held a poster she'd made with photos of Peerybingle and Belle. She wished that her two favorite horses could have come for the blessing too. *But they're here in spirit!* she thought.

Katie smiled, remembering back to the day last spring when Patrick found his pet at the creek. So much had happened since then! When little Francis the frog had almost ruined the baptism of their adopted baby sister, Hoa Hong, Mom and Dad had volunteered the whole family for the St. Anne's Cleaning Team.

Now, the Brady family spent a few hours at church every Saturday. And some pretty amazing things had happened. Patrick and Katie had gone on a few adventures, learned some secrets about

St. Anne's, and were closer than ever. Patrick didn't even complain when it was time to go to church anymore.

As Mrs. Brady stood behind the twins and Dr. Brady chased Hoa Hong around the blacktop, Fr. Miguel explained the connection between St. Francis's feast day and the blessing of the animals.

"Today, we celebrate an amazing saint," the priest said over the sound of meowing and barking and even the oinking of Maria's pet pot-bellied pig, Princess.

"St. Francis of Assisi loved all of God's creatures so much that he even called them Brother and Sister. Today, in his honor and out of praise for our Creator, we gather together to bless our friends, the animals."

*Ribbit*, croaked Francis the frog in agreement.

"Amen!" Hoa Hong yelled in her loud toddler's voice, making everyone smile.

Katie and Patrick weren't embarrassed about their little sister's rowdy prayer. They'd waited so long to meet their adopted sibling. She had been born in Vietnam, but now she was part of their family, and the twins let her get away with a lot.

At the front of the crowd, Erin and Gregory, the class officers for Mr. Birks's class, took turns reading a special "Canticle" prayer that St. Francis had written:

*Praised be You, my Lord, with all Your creatures...* they recited together.

Patrick and Katie, who could almost always read each other's minds, smiled at the sight of the class "cool girl" and the holiest brainiac of St. Anne's praying together in front of the whole school. Nearby, Lily, the newest girl at St. Anne's, led the school in the closing song. "Make Me a Channel of Your Peace," Lily sang in her sweet voice. All around her, dogs, cats, hamsters, and even Mrs. Ray's pet goat chimed in.

Only one tough kid and his bulldog stood silent, their eyes dark and cloudy.

# ▲ Chapter Two ▲

When the Brady van pulled into the St. Anne's parking lot the next morning, Katie and Patrick were shocked by what they saw.

"*Yikes!*" Patrick said, rolling down the window on his side of the car to get a better look at the side of the old stone church. "What happened?"

As Mom pulled into a parking spot, the twins saw several of their classmates standing with the principal, Sr. Margaret, Mr. Birks, and Fr. Miguel in the Mary Garden next to the church. Everyone was staring up at the big stained-glass window, pointing to a large hole.

In his hand, Fr. Miguel held a brick. As he talked to the principal and the teacher, he passed it from one hand to the other. Then he set the brick on the ground and pointed back up at the window, waving his arms as he talked.

"Wow," Katie exclaimed. "It looks like the St. Francis window got broken!"

"Oh dear," Mom sighed, unloading Hoa Hong from her car seat. "That window is more than a hundred years old. How sad!"

Patrick and Katie ran across the parking lot to join their classmates and teacher. Erin, Maria, and Lily were huddled in a circle, their voices low as they tried to guess what could have happened. Fr. Miguel raised both hands and whistled.

"Kids," said the priest, trying to calm the loud students, "I think we need to take a minute and pray together for the person who did this."

"They're going to *need* prayers when they get caught!" Pedro, the class clown, joked.

"Yeah," Erin agreed. "Who would do something like this? What a loser!"

As the kids began to grumble, the priest whistled again.

"OK, OK," he assured them. "You're mad. I'll admit it, I'm upset too. But whoever did this was also mad about something, and maybe still is. Let's pray for them and for wisdom about how we're going to get this problem fixed. Sr. Margaret, would you lead us in prayer?"

So there, in the middle of the rose bushes and next to the Mary statue, the students of St. Anne's joined together in a Hail Mary. Then they headed quietly back across the parking lot to class.

Katie and Patrick settled into their desks next to each other in the second row. Mr. Birks stood at his laptop next to the smartboard, typing. The twins had been excited when they found out that Mr. Birks was going to be their teacher since they'd known him from their father's basketball team.

They watched as he flipped on the smartboard, which read: Next report assignment is St. Francis of Assisi.

"Come on, Coach," Patrick groaned, calling Mr. Birks by his popular nickname. "Seriously, we *just* finished our science reports!"

"Then it's the perfect time for a new mission!" Mr. Birks replied with a smile in his eyes.

# ▲ Chapter Three ▲

"*Let's go!*" Patrick shouted over the shrill ringing of the lunch bell. Across the parking lot, the old church bells were chiming nine times to remind the St. Anne's neighborhood that it was time to pray the noon Angelus. Noon was the moment every day when both bells at St. Anne's went off at once. As the loud church bells rang in the background, they were drowned out by the electronic school bells.

"Soccer or basketball?" asked Gregory, heading toward the ball basket in the corner of the classroom.

"Neither, for you, *dweeb!*" grunted Peter, grabbing a football. "We thought we'd use you as our tackling dummy today..."

Shoving Gregory out of the way with a snort, Peter looked over his shoulder to six much smaller members of the St. Anne's flag football team. The sporty kids laughed at Gregory.

"Come on, Gregory," called Patrick, trying to make the tallest but least athletic kid in the class feel better. "We need you on our team!"

Patrick strapped his flags around his waist and grabbed his lunchbox before heading to the metal lunch tables next to the football field. He landed on the bench between Pedro and Gregory, directly across from his sister.

Katie and her friends were caught up in a conversation of their own. They barely noticed Patrick and his buddies swoop in and wolf down their sandwiches. Katie watched Patrick lead Gregory and Pedro to the field.

"Who do you think did it?" Maria asked. "I wonder if they caught him on the security cameras."

"How do you know it was a 'him'?" Erin challenged her.

"Did you see the size of that hole?" Lily exclaimed. "And that brick that Fr. Miguel had? I mean, you'd have to be pretty strong to throw a brick so high!"

Katie listened to her friends but kept quiet.

Her eyes were on Peter and his posse, cracking jokes at the end of the metal benches. One of the boys guzzled his milk, burped loudly, and accepted a bunch of high fives from the kids sitting around him. For a second, Katie's eyes met Peter's.

"Gross!" yelled Erin. "Why don't you guys get outta here?!"

Suddenly, Peter dropped his sandwich and shoved the rest of his food onto the ground. As he marched angrily toward the girls, Katie stood, trying to be brave. Next to her, Lily stood up too. Katie pushed her red braids behind her and stood as tall as she could.

"You got a problem?" Peter challenged them, looking at Erin. "You're just too perfect to be around someone like me, aren't you?"

"C'mon, Peter," Lily said, putting her hand on Peter's strong shoulder.

"Back off, Lily!" Peter shot back.

Katie stepped between Lily and Peter, summoning her courage.

"Peter, why don't we…" she started, using the voice Dad always used when the twins were starting to argue.

Patrick, who had suddenly rushed back to the lunch benches to stand with his twin, interrupted her.

"What's your problem, Peter?" Patrick asked, his voice cracking a little bit. He and Katie might battle occasionally, but the Brady twins always stood up for each other. "You gonna fight with a girl?"

"No problem, Brady," Peter snarled, sounding almost as mean as his bulldog. Behind Patrick, Mr. Birks was heading toward them. "Let's just take this to the football field. We'll see who's got a problem then…"

With his friends in tow, Peter turned his back and slumped away.

But not before both Patrick and Katie noticed the dark look in his eyes.

# ▲ Chapter Four ▲

"So, what do you think his deal is?" Patrick whispered to Katie in the back seat of the van. They were headed to what Mom called "Friday afternoon fun"—a circuit where Mom would drop Katie off at Reinhard's Stables for riding lessons, Patrick at the karate dojo, and then head to baby gym for an hour with Hoa Hong.

In the front of the van, Mom was busy singing "We Will Rock You" with the twins' little sister, who seemed to be going through a major classic rock phase.

"I mean, he's always been a tough kid," Patrick said. "But lately he's been extra mean."

"I know!" Katie agreed. "Yesterday, it was like he was just looking to get into a fight with someone."

By the time they'd arrived at Reinhard's, the twins had a theory about the broken St. Francis window. Everyone in Mr. Birks's class was still trying to figure out who could have ruined such an old and important part of the church's history. They all wanted someone—anyone—to blame.

"You talk to Lily at riding, and I'll check with Pedro at karate," Patrick said.

"Then we'll compare notes afterward," Katie said, "so that we can talk to Fr. Miguel at Cleaning Team tomorrow."

Thirty minutes later, Katie was atop her new favorite horse Peerybingle while Lily cantered nearby on Belle.

"So, what do you think?" she called to Lily. "Was it Peter?"

A few miles away, Patrick was having the same conversation with Pedro. "What's up with Peter, dude?" he asked his buddy at the first water break. "Do you think he did it?"

An hour later, back in the van, the twins compared notes.

"He lives within walking distance of St. Anne's," Patrick whispered. "I was there for his birthday party last year, and you can hear the Angelus bells from his backyard."

"So, he definitely could have snuck out and done it!" Katie said, just a little too loudly.

"What's up, kids?" asked Mom from the front seat. She turned down the music and looked back at the redheaded pair.

"Oh, nothing, Mom!" The twins said at once.

In the front seat, Mom stayed quiet, but she was definitely paying attention.

# ▲ Chapter Five ▲

The following day, the Bradys' red van pulled into the St. Anne's parking lot fifteen minutes before noon. The twins grabbed their backpacks and sprinted to the big iron doors of the church. Katie had never seen Patrick so excited to get to church for their volunteer Cleaning Team shift.

They both hurried up toward the altar to find Fr. Miguel and Mrs. Danks, the Cleaning Team captain. They pointed up to the broken window.

"We've been thinking about who could have done it," Patrick said.

"And we're pretty sure we know," said Katie.

"Kids," Fr. Miguel said in a hushed voice, "I have a meeting with the parish leadership team and Bishop Robert after we finish here. We're working on our plans for the window. Right now, let's just focus on getting this place all fixed up for Bishop's visit!"

The twins knew that the bishop was very busy and couldn't make his way to St. Anne's often. They decided to focus on getting the church clean. They could talk to Fr. Miguel later.

"Katie, my darling," Mrs. Danks said in her Irish accent, while she looked at her clipboard of jobs, "please take this cloth and polish and see to the Tabernacle."

"And Patrick," Fr. Miguel chimed in, "why don't you take my vacuum and head over to the aisle on the right side of the nave? I'd like for you to clean up the area under the St. Francis window. We want to make sure there aren't any small pieces of glass on the rug before people come for Mass tomorrow. And watch out over there, buddy."

"Watch out?" Patrick asked, looking at the priest.

"Don't cut yourself," Fr. Miguel said.

*Vacuuming, again?* Patrick thought as he pushed the heavy vacuum. He'd just had to do his least favorite chore at home this morning, and here he was again. *Twice in one day...*

Patrick looked up at the fractured window, realizing that he'd never really spent much time examining it. Just looking at that damage made him furious.

His eyes moved from the huge, gaping hole to the window's bottom right corner. Black numbers in the glass announced the year St. Anne's had been built.

Patrick fired up the vacuum and began to push it along the stone wall. Near the end of the window, he spotted a dark stone on a low part of the wall. It looked older and was bigger than the others. Across the stone, four large letters were carved: *MCCV.*

Patrick flipped off the loud vacuum. As he looked at the mysterious letters, the first of the nine noontime Angelus bells began to chime, calling the parish and neighborhood to prayer.

*Clang, clang, clang...*

"MCCV?" Patrick rubbed his fingers over the stone's surface as a second set of three chimes rang out.

Overhead, sun poured through the hole in the window as the last three chimes rang. Patrick's mind raced to figure out what the letters could mean. Then he felt an intense rush of cold wind.

And suddenly, the ground began to rumble and everything became a blur.

# ▲ Chapter Six ▲

Feeling like he'd just gotten off a crazy roller coaster, Patrick stood upright. One last, hollow-sounding chime from a bell rang out. He brushed dust from the knees of his jeans and tried to steady his shaking legs.

Patrick looked around in every direction. He was no longer in the nave of St. Anne's. He reached out, touching the light-colored stones of the wall next to him.

"Wow! I did it! I chime traveled!" Patrick said excitedly when he realized that he was now outside. The air around him felt cold and damp. The night sky was dark, and he smelled something cooking nearby. "Where am I?" he asked, to no one in particular. "And *when* am I?"

He was standing in a narrow, winding alleyway. It looked almost like a road, but Patrick saw no cars. The alley smelled like a mix of pizza and animals. He looked for clues that might tell him where and when he had landed in time.

"Now what?" Patrick wondered out loud, looking down at the jeans and hoodie he was wearing. "No Francis with me this time around," he whispered. He missed his pet frog already!

Ever since he and Francis the frog had mysteriously been transported to Ireland and met St. Patrick last school year, Patrick had been obsessed with the idea of time travel. He'd read every book on the topic in the St. Anne's school library. He and Katie had even ridden their bikes to the County Library every week during the summer, in search of clues about what they had experienced.

Though the Brady twins didn't have any solid answers, they had a few ideas.

They guessed that their mysterious "missions" had been started by the ringing of the Angelus bells at St. Anne's. They also figured out that they had zero control over when it would happen. The twins had tried to chime travel again. They made sure they were inside the church when the bells were chiming at noon. They tried to go back to the exact spots in the church that had mysteriously transported them the first time.

But nothing had happened…and they eventually gave up. Now, though, Patrick found himself in a new place and time again. How had it happened?

Toward one end of the stone street, Patrick heard boys' voices. He considered running in the

opposite direction, up the small hill. But that way led to shadows of what looked like a stone fort or castle. Patrick froze, trying to figure out which way to go. As he hesitated, the rowdy voices grew closer.

Before he could come up with a plan, a small pack of boys around his age approached him.

"*Chi è?*" one of them said, circling Patrick and looking at his clothing. Patrick noticed that their clothes were very different and old-fashioned. They were all at least a few inches taller than he was, and their eyes were mean. He shivered, more out of fear than from the cold. He'd met some bullies on his last chime travel mission to Ireland and was pretty sure these boys weren't going to be friendly.

"I… I'm…" Patrick stuttered. The boys circled closer. One of them flipped the hood of Patrick's sweatshirt from behind. He felt breath on his face as the tall boy leaned in to have a closer look at Patrick's red hair.

Around the corner came a young man, singing happily. With a smile on he face, the man called out to the pack of boys, his tone joking. Whatever he said caused the gang to take a step back from Patrick.

Before Patrick knew what was happening, the friendly young man flung a beautiful cloak around his shoulders and pulled him away from the bullies.

"*Andiamo!*" he said with a smile. "Let's get you to my father's store so you can find some better clothing. These are such strange rags you're wearing!"

Patrick followed the friendly man to a clothing store with the name "Bernardone" on the door, happily leaving the gang of glaring boys behind.

# ▲ Chapter Seven ▲

"Welcome to Bernardone's!" his new friend said.

"*Grazie!*" Patrick said, surprising himself. He marveled that he was having a conversation in Italian.

*This must be part of the chime traveling!* Patrick thought.

A lovely woman entered the shop from a room in the back. "Has my Giovanni Francesco brought another of his poor friends into our store to be fed and clothed?"

"*Ciao, Mamma!* My little friend," he turned to Patrick. "I have forgotten my manners and have not even asked your name!"

"I'm Patrick." He was beginning to feel at ease after such a warm welcome.

"Ah, Patrick, a fine but unusual name in this village! I was named Giovanni at birth by my beautiful mamma, Lady Pica. But my father loves the French and their fine goods and food. So, please, call me as he does—Francesco. Francis for short!" He smiled widely.

*Francis? Could it be Pope Francis?* Patrick thought. But this brown-haired young man looked nothing like the famous pope for whom his pet frog had been named. He didn't look much older than Mr. Birks, and he was thin and strong with dark, wavy hair. He was definitely shorter than Pope Francis, and much younger too!

"Thank you, Mr. Francis. Thank you, Lady Pica," Patrick said, trying to be polite. "Do you have a telephone I could use? I need to call my mom."

"A telephone?" Francis and his mother asked.

Lady Pica said, "We have no such 'telephone.' But we can help you get a cart to carry you to your mamma once you have dined with us."

No phone? A cart? And speaking Italian? Patrick had to keep himself from shouting his excitement out loud as he began to put the pieces together. *Is it possible?* he wondered, looking at Francis. *Could this be the famous saint?*

Realizing that he was starving, he decided to accept their kindness. "Will your dad be here for dinner?" he asked.

"Not tonight," Francis answered. "He is on another of his trips, purchasing cloth from distant merchants to sell here in our store. He wants to be the most wealthy and respected merchant in all the world!"

"One day soon, my son," smiled Pica, "and all of this will be yours. I will prepare our dinner, and we shall dine with Patrick as our guest."

When his mother left the room, Francis let out a loud sigh.

"What's wrong?" Patrick asked, seeing a tear roll down his new friend's face.

"It is very hard to explain," Francis said, absentmindedly folding some deep blue cloth. "I don't share my father's dreams for my life. I'm a changed man. I have new dreams."

"Like what?" Patrick asked. He wanted to understand how his new friend was feeling, especially because he'd been so happy just a few minutes ago.

"My whole life, I dreamed of being a famous knight," Francis said. "I went off to war, but we were defeated, captured, and put in prison. By the time I was finally able to come home, I was sick almost to the point of death."

"Wow, that's crazy!" Patrick was immediately glued to the story. Knights and battles and prison? How exciting!

"Eventually, I recovered. I even tried to go to another war. But something had changed within me. I went to Rome. I learned so many lessons there, including a great love for the poor and the needy. I hadn't realized before that so many people aren't as blessed as my family. We have so much that we could share with those who struggle and go hungry..."

Francis stared off into space. "My parents want me to marry a girl from a good family. But I have found my bride," he said. "Her name is Lady Poverty!"

"*Lady Poverty*? Weird name! Does she live around here? Why won't your father like her?" Patrick had noticed how close Francis was with his mom. But he seemed to have problems with his dad.

Francis smiled at Patrick's eager questions. "Lady Poverty is not a person, but I have met her in the faces of those most in need. I give them the scraps from our table; I give them my hat, my belt, or even the shirt off my back. But somehow, it's never enough," Francis's eyes lit up again. "God is calling me to give more!"

# ▲ Chapter Eight ▲

"Before you return to your family," Lady Pica said to Patrick the next morning, "I thought you might like to take a hike with Francesco to see a bit of our home since it is so different from your own."

Patrick had told them all about his family and St. Anne's at dinner the night before. He could tell they were amazed by his story. But he was grateful, too, because they also believed him. Before going to bed, they agreed they would find a way to help him get back to his family.

A hike might be a good way to learn more about where—and exactly when—he was. But Patrick wasn't in a big rush to get home. He was pretty sure he was hanging out with St. Francis, which was super cool. He couldn't wait to learn more about Francis's home and this amazing time in history. Spending a day with Francis might help Patrick confirm his suspicions about who he was, too.

After a breakfast of delicious, crusty bread and dried meats, the two set off down the hill and away from the village center.

"I love to get out of the busyness of the village," Francis told Patrick as they hiked through a wheat field. "God feels closer out here in the middle of the olive trees and beneath the open sky!"

"I know what you mean!" Patrick agreed. "Back home, the creek is one of my favorite spots. It's so easy to feel close to God out there in the middle of the trees with the crickets chirping. That's where I found Francis!"

"Francis?" the young man asked, a sparkle in his eyes.

"My pet frog," Patrick said with a giggle. "I named him after someone special!"

Francis joined in Patrick's laughter, even hopping a few times as he considered a frog with his own name. "I love frogs, and crickets, too!" he smiled.

*Loves animals?* Patrick added this to his mental list of evidence.

Hiking down the gently sloping hill, he turned and looked back toward the village. Near the top, he could see the castle he'd spotted yesterday. "Francis," he asked, "what are those big buildings in the village?"

"Such a sight from here!" Francis said, turning to take in the view with Patrick. "From this spot, you see both the fort of Rocca Maggiore and the San Rufino Cathedral where I was baptized. Two of the finest buildings in Assisi!"

"Assisi?" Patrick shouted, turning again to look at the dark-haired young man. "Francis? Assisi? You're Francis of Assisi!" He had almost said the word *saint*, but something stopped him. Maybe the saints he met weren't supposed to know they were going to be saints.

*I was right!* Patrick thought to himself. He had been putting all the clues about Francis together in his head. He couldn't wait to see what else he was going to learn on this mission!

Francis gave him a funny look but seemed to decide not to push it. "I've passed this place a few times," he said a minute later. He pointed to a crumbling old stone building. "My heart's calling me to stop and pray here today. Will you join me?"

"Sure!" Patrick said. "What is this place? It looks pretty broken down. Is it safe to go inside?"

"This," Francis pointed to the stone structure, "is a chapel. But it's been forgotten. There's no one here now except a lonely priest who lives on the charity of others."

Patrick pulled the creaky door of the building open. "Wow, what a mess!"

They walked into the dark, damp structure. Patrick heard the sound of bugs and birds chirping and cooing in the corners. It had a weird smell, too. Cobwebs tickled his face. Something scurried across the floor toward them. Francis bent and scooped the tiny creature into his hands.

"A new friend! What shall we call you?" Francis asked the little mouse. After thinking for a moment, he said, "I present to you Brother Bernard!"

Patrick reached out, happy to have a chance to hold the small creature. "*Ciao*, Bernard!" he whispered with a smile. Somehow this little guy made the creepy chapel feel more comfortable. "Would you like to pray with me?"

The small room was almost black in the darkness. Patrick followed Francis and knelt down on the cold rock floor. Above the simple wooden altar, a cross hung from the ceiling. Patrick thought about how different this cross looked from the crucifix at St. Anne's. This one was wooden and had faded color paintings of different saints. From the center of the crucifix, Patrick saw Jesus look down at him. Jesus's eyes were painted wide open.

They prayed quietly for several minutes. Then suddenly, the silence was broken by a voice, unlike anything Patrick had ever heard before.

"Francis, go and repair my church which is falling into ruin."

Patrick's heart beat wildly. He looked at Francis, kneeling next to him. The young man's eyes were glued to the cross.

"Did you hear that?" Patrick asked, wondering if he had imagined the voice. Francis seemed totally caught up in prayer and didn't answer.

Patrick had never been so sure of anything. "I heard a whisper, coming right from the middle of the chapel, from that old cross. From Jesus!"

Suddenly Francis stood, making the Sign of the Cross. He pulled a small purse from his pocket and took several coins out. He left them on the corner of the altar.

"For the priest," Francis explained, "so that he can buy some oil and properly light this holy place."

"And then what?" Patrick asked. He wasn't ready to leave so quickly after hearing a mysterious voice! "You heard that voice, right? We can't just rush out!"

"We have plans to make," Francis said, heading to the door. "We have work to do here!"

# ⏶ Chapter Nine ⏶

On the way back, Patrick asked, "Where are we going now?"

Francis paused and smiled.

"I heard the voice of Jesus Christ, calling me from that precious cross," Francis said. "Christ has given this knight his marching orders—to repair the church of San Damiano."

"You mean, like, fix it up?" Patrick asked.

"Exactly!" Francis responded, hurrying toward Bernardone's.

"But how? Where will you get tools and wood and stuff?" Patrick asked. He remembered how messed up the old chapel was. From his shoulder, little Bernard squeaked. Patrick let the mouse nuzzle his finger, grateful for his new friend. He imagined that Francis the frog would love Bernard, too!

"I will go the city of Foligno to do business," Francis explained. "You and Bernard can travel along with me. From the city, we will return you to your parents."

"Sounds like a plan." He didn't want to argue with Francis. But he also knew he wasn't in a hurry to get home yet. "Feel like going on a mission, Bernard?"

*Squeak*!

Francis entered the store and found several bolts of deep scarlet cloth. He gathered them into a large satchel.

"Doesn't this fabric belong to your dad?" Patrick asked. "Should you ask him?" Francis didn't answer, and Patrick could tell from the way he was rushing that his father, Signor Bernardone, was not going to be happy when he came back to the store.

Outside, Francis found his horse and climbed onto his back. He pulled Patrick up into the saddle behind him. They rode ten miles to Foligno and quickly found a buyer for the cloth.

"But we still don't have enough to rebuild the church…" Francis sighed, counting his coins.

Then he looked up at his horse. His face brightened. "I think I know a way to find the rest of the money we need!" Francis turned to the beautiful horse with tears in his eyes. "I will miss you, my brother. You have served me so bravely," he said, petting the horse's dark mane. "But we will be together in spirit!"

An hour later, Francis, Patrick, and little Bernard were walking the ten miles back toward Assisi.

The tiny mouse scurried ahead of them on the path. Every so often, he would circle back, stand on his hind legs, and insist that Patrick carry him for a while.

As they walked under the bright sun, Patrick and Francis made plans.

"Isn't your dad going to be super mad that you sold all that stuff? Especially his horse?" Patrick asked.

Francis answered as if he were practicing what he would tell his angry father. "That was a valuable warhorse," he said. "But I am not going off to war. The money we made might be enough to buy the mortar and tools we need. Surely my father won't be too angry when he learns of our plan to help so many people by repairing the chapel."

"Does your dad get angry easily?" Patrick asked.

"He is a good man," Francis said. "But his whole life is business and money and power. He wants those same things for me. He wants me to be a success and to have a fine life. My father doesn't understand that what I really want is to give my life to Christ and to help others, especially the poor. I sometimes wonder if he'll ever accept me."

Patrick looked at Francis. He seemed more sad than afraid.

"We should probably decide how we will get you home to your family now, Patrick," he said kindly.

"Can't I stay and help you?" Patrick definitely wanted to stay with Francis and see what would happen next. "Dad lets me help him with all kinds of projects at home. I'm actually pretty good with tools."

"If you don't think your family would mind, I'm sure you'll be a great help. With the money we earned and two strong men," Francis said, patting Patrick's shoulder, "we should be off to a good start."

*Squeak!*

"Don't forget about Bernard!" Patrick giggled.

"And God will provide the rest!" Francis agreed with a smile.

As they approached the little chapel again, Patrick thought that for someone who had just sold everything but the pants and shoes he was wearing, Francis seemed very happy.

But when they met the chapel's caretaker, the man tried to turn them away.

"Francis," Fr. Antonio warned them, "your father is back from his travels. He's heard what you've done. He's furious that you've taken cloth from the store, and the horse, too!"

Patrick stopped in his tracks. In the distance, they could hear the sound of hooves thundering. Pietro Bernardone and his men were galloping toward San Damiano. Bernard quivered on Patrick's shoulder. Francis had told Patrick enough about his father that Patrick knew Signor Bernardone's anger would be formidable.

But Francis was already prepared for this. "Come," he said, "I know a safe place where we can stay for a while until my father is less angry." Then Francis took out the money that he had earned for selling the horse and cloth. He tossed the small moneybag into a dark corner of the chapel.

As they hurried away from San Damiano, Patrick whispered to the church mouse, "Maybe we should have gone home when we had the chance, Bernard!"

# ⏶ Chapter Ten ⏶

"Why doesn't Fr. Antonio want us to fix San Damiano?" Patrick asked.

"My father is so powerful that he often frightens people," Francis answered. Patrick's mind immediately rushed to Peter, the most powerful kid he knew. He was the biggest kid in class, so he could easily frighten other kids when he wanted to. Peter wasn't really a mean kid. But something was definitely making him angry lately.

"I believe Fr. Antonio will change his mind in time," Francis said.

"So what do we do now?" Patrick didn't want to admit it to Francis, but he was scared, too.

"Now, we go to the pit."

"*The pit*? That doesn't sound too great."

"It is a safe place," Francis assured him, "and this will give us time to prepare for what's to come."

At first, Patrick thought that the "pit," which was actually more of an underground cave, was dark and scary. The gloominess and constant cold made him fear that he would never see his family again. He missed Katie, and wondered what she would do in this situation. He missed Hoa Hong's happy little laugh. He missed shooting hoops with Dad and Mom's cooking, too. But having Francis around was always fun. Even in the dark pit, Francis stayed positive. He always reminded Patrick that God was with them.

One morning as they shared some dry bread, Patrick told Francis about Peter.

"There's this kid, Peter, at school," Patrick said. "He's always been tough, but lately he has been so mean. Everyone at school's pretty afraid of him. And someone threw a brick through one of the windows at church. Fr. Miguel said whoever did it was mad at something." Patrick shrugged. He was hesitant to say out loud what he was thinking. *Peter has seemed mad lately.*

Francis listened, nodding silently.

"It just seems like maybe, because he was so mad, that maybe he..."

Francis interrupted him. "We don't know what's in Peter's heart," he said. "It isn't your job to try and figure out why Peter does what he does. Only God knows what's in Peter's heart. Your job is to be his brother, his friend. Your job is to help him find peace."

*Help Peter find peace?* Patrick thought. *Maybe he's mad because something's really wrong.* He hadn't really considered that before.

"Yuck!" Patrick yelled as a creepy bug crawled across his foot.

Francis picked up the cockroach, cradled it in his hands for a moment, and said, "Good morning, Sister." He moved the bug to a safe corner of the pit. "It will be a bit more peaceful for you over here!"

Patrick soon learned that, along with being a great singer, Francis was an amazing storyteller, too.

"Tell me another one!" Patrick begged many times.

Francis acted out different Bible stories Patrick remembered hearing at Mass. Francis became Moses, crouching to talk to the burning bush, or Noah, leading the animals two by two onto the ark.

"Let my people go!" Francis shouted another time as he told the story of Pharaoh and the Israelites.

"Walk on the water again!" Patrick asked another day. He loved the way his friend brought the voice of Jesus to life in the stories. Francis helped Patrick see Jesus feeding five thousand with only a few loaves and fishes. He became Joseph hearing and trusting God's angel. He was Peter and Paul spreading the Gospel after Jesus ascended to heaven.

"Listening to you teach about the Bible is like watching a movie!" Patrick laughed.

Francis didn't know what a movie was, but he knew it was a compliment. "I'd love to spend my life alone in silent prayer," Francis said, "but God calls us to share his Good News. And people are hungry to know God's Word!"

While Patrick was eager to get out of the cave, Bernard the mouse seemed right at home. He played games with them, and even snuck out to the streets of Assisi at night to find snacks. More than any of them, the little church mouse felt comfortable in the pit.

# ▲ Chapter Eleven ▲

"It is time to face my father," Francis finally said one day.

The announcement made Patrick nervous, but he trusted his friend. He knew Francis had been praying about it since the day they arrived in the pit. It was time to go.

When they arrived at the store that afternoon, Pietro Bernardone was furious.

"Father—" Francis started, but he never got a chance to finish. Pietro Bernardone grabbed him by the arm and dragged him to his room.

"Wait!" Patrick called, shocked.

Pietro Bernardone pushed Francis into the room and slammed the door, locking him inside.

"You will stay there until you come to your senses!" he growled.

Patrick stood with Bernard, wondering what to do next. Pietro Bernardone's anger scared him, even though right now, he looked sad more than angry. Still, Patrick was nervous. Then, a hand touched his shoulder lightly. He looked up into the sad eyes of Francis's mother, Lady Pica.

"Come, let us have tea." She directed Patrick into the kitchen. "You are free to stay with us and visit with Francis."

Patrick asked, "What will happen to Francis? We're planning to repair the chapel at San Damiano."

"My husband, like many in Assisi, thinks our Francis has gone crazy," said Lady Pica. "We must give Pietro a bit of time to calm down. And perhaps Francis will change his mind."

But Lady Pica understood her son better than anyone. She knew he was determined as well as patient. It wasn't likely he'd change his mind.

"Lady Pica," Patrick said, his fingers crumbling up the cookie on his plate, "Francis has been called by God."

She raised her eyebrows, waiting for him to continue.

"I was with him. I heard Jesus speak to him." It was one thing to admit to hearing God's voice that day in the chapel when the only other person around had heard it too. But now, telling Lady Pica, Patrick felt nervous. Would she believe him? Would people think he was crazy like they thought Francis was crazy?

Lady Pica was quiet for a moment. Then she sighed again, but this time, she was smiling.

"Thank you, Patrick. You are a good friend to my Francesco."

A couple of days later, when Pietro was away selling silk, Lady Pica and Patrick visited Francis in his room. Francis was kneeling by his bed in prayer when they entered.

"Francesco," Lady Pica said, "can't we please go back to the way things were in the past?"

Patrick and Bernard stayed quiet, but they both knew what Francis would say to his mother. They watched as Francis stood and faced her. There was a sparkle of determination in his eye, but he looked a little sad, too. He took her hand and kissed the back of her fingers.

"I have work to do, Mother."

She clasped her son's hands in hers and, after a long moment, nodded.

"I've prepared a basket of food for you," she said, unlocking the door to Francis's room. Before Francis and Patrick left the house, Lady Pica took Francis's face in her hands. Her eyes were wet with tears. She kissed his forehead. "Peace and all good, my dear Francesco. My prayers are with you."

# ▲ Chapter Twelve ▲

With Bernard tucked safely into Patrick's pocket, they ran down the hill to San Damiano.

Fr. Antonio met them at the door.

"I see you are serious this time," the priest said, smiling as he welcomed them back into the chapel.

Patrick and Francis began sketching plans on the dirty floor of the tiny chapel. They had been working for a few hours when they heard furious yelling and the sound of horses galloping in their direction.

"Your father!" Patrick said. He stood up, panicked. "Where should we hide?"

"We will not hide," Francis said. He went to the corner of the chapel and collected the money he had thrown there. Francis walked outside boldly and calmly went to face his father.

Francis held out the pouch when his father's horse stopped in front of him. "This belongs to you."

Pietro grabbed the small purse. He glared down at his son. "I will be back," he said, and then rode angrily away. "And the police will be with me!"

His father tried to have Francis arrested, but the police would not come.

"We will not take him to jail," the police captain said. "This is a matter for Bishop Guido to decide."

The matter was taken to the bishop, and it was decided that Francis would be put on trial. His father was pleased, certain that the bishop would side with him. But Francis did not seem worried.

"God has called me, Patrick," he said. "I trust him."

Soon, the time came for Francis's trial. Francis stood in the center of Assisi's square beside Bishop Guido. Patrick shivered in the cold. Pietro Bernardone paced angrily, yelling his complaints to the bishop.

"His actions have cost me a fortune!" Pietro said.

But before Bishop Guido could answer, Francis—who had already given all his money to Pietro—stood and took off all his clothing and gave it to his father.

Standing humbly before the crowd in the cold, Francis spoke loudly. "Until today, I called Pietro Bernardone my father. But today, I give him not only my money, but my clothes, too. From now on, I can honestly say, 'Our Father who art in heaven.' As of today, God is my only father!"

Everyone was stunned, including Pietro. Bishop Guido took off his own cloak and wrapped it around Francis. For a moment, the young man looked like a sad little boy as he gazed at the man who had raised him. Patrick thought of his own father, and his heart hurt for Francis.

Pietro Bernardone took one last look at his son, then turned and walked away.

# ▲ Chapter Thirteen ▲

After the trial, Patrick heard one of the citizens of Assisi ask his neighbor, "How could such a rich young man just give up everything?" Even though Patrick knew it had been hard for Francis to leave his family, he also knew that Francis had not given up what mattered most to him.

Bishop Guido told his helpers to bring Francis some clothing. Francis put on a scratchy brown robe and tied a rope around his waist, smiling. The bishop's helper found chalk and drew a cross on Francis's robe.

"You need to leave Assisi until your father calms down," Bishop Guido said.

Francis nodded. "Patrick and I can go visit my friends in Gubbio."

Gubbio was a place where many sick and poor people lived. Bishop Guido knew that Francis wanted to take care of them. "When you arrive," the bishop told them, "find my friend Federico. He will give you food and a place to stay."

They spent the next day hiking to Gubbio. As they walked, Patrick noticed birds flocking above them, as though they were following the three travelers.

"Thank you for your song, my brothers and sisters," Francis shouted to the sky. "You make our journey a pleasure!"

Patrick laughed. Francis always spoke to every animal they met!

"What's Gubbio like?" Patrick asked.

"It's a special place. We will meet people called 'lepers' who are very poor and sick, but also very kind."

Patrick remembered Mr. Birks teaching them about leprosy, which was now called Hansen's disease. He'd read in the Bible about Jesus and lepers, too. Dad had taught him and Katie that now there was medicine to cure this terrible sickness. But in Francis's time, the people with this disease were outcasts. Everyone was afraid to be around them or to touch them.

When they arrived, many people ran out to welcome them. Patrick saw that the lepers had terrible sores on their faces and bodies. Their clothes were ragged and torn.

He suddenly understood why people used to stay away from them. "Will they hurt us?" Patrick asked. "They look pretty sick, and they smell terrible! Is it OK to touch them?"

"These families need someone to care for them," Francis said. "But do not be afraid. God is with us." He smiled and ran forward to meet the crowds.

"They are so happy to see Francis!" Patrick smiled to Bernard. The little mouse squeaked. The excited crowd led them to Federico.

"*Benvenuti!*" the kind man said, welcoming them into his simple house. "Bishop Guido sent a message that you would join us. You are welcome!"

Over dinner, Federico told Francis and Patrick about a terrible pack of wolves that had taken over Gubbio. "The largest," Federico said, "is the most vicious creature we have ever seen. He kills anyone who comes near him!" Bernard sat on the bench next to Francis. His whiskers twitched as he listened to the conversation.

"We will have to see about this," said Francis. "I must talk to Brother Wolf and learn why he is so angry."

Bernard stood on his back legs bravely. He was ready to face the Wolf of Gubbio!

Patrick wasn't so sure about going to talk to a wolf, but he had watched Francis with so many other animals and insects. His friend had a special way of communicating with them.

"If anyone can calm down a vicious wolf, it's Francis!" Patrick said to Federico and Bernard.

The next morning, all of Gubbio stood watching as Francis walked outside the gates toward the den of wolves. Patrick, Bernard, Federico, and a few strong men followed Francis until he told them to stop and wait.

Francis walked calmly to the den. Patrick thought the wolves looked like the meanest dogs he'd ever seen. He couldn't help but think of Peter and Leo.

Suddenly, the biggest, meanest wolf of all ran straight toward Francis. Perched on Patrick's shoulder, Bernard squeaked a courageous warning.

But Francis stopped and faced the approaching wolf head-on. He raised his hand and made a sign of the cross in the air. The giant wolf stopped instantly and laid down at Francis's feet facing him.

"Brother Wolf," Francis said to the now calm beast, "you have been terrorizing Gubbio. Everyone is so afraid of you!"

The wolf looked up into Francis's eyes.

"Brother Wolf, I come to you in peace. If you will stop attacking my friends, we will forgive you. My friends from Gubbio promise to feed and care for you. Will you promise to make peace with them?" Francis put his hand out toward the wolf.

Patrick couldn't believe what happened next! The huge wolf stood and put its big black paw into Francis's hand. Then Francis said, "Come with me, Brother Wolf, and I will introduce you to my friends! They will care for you."

The big wolf followed Francis and his friends through the gates and back into Gubbio. Francis said to the crowd, "This is Brother Wolf. He has promised to make peace with you. I ask that you feed and care for him as one of God's creatures."

As the giant wolf turned to Francis and again lifted his paw into the man's hand for all of Gubbio to see, the crowd burst into cheers.

# ▲ Chapter Fourteen ▲

Francis, Patrick, and little Bernard stayed with the families of Gubbio long enough to make sure that the peace Francis had made with the wolves would last. Francis told Patrick, "Brother Wolf is just like our other friends in Gubbio. He is one of God's creatures like Brother Bernard, or you, or me. God wants us to love one another and to take care of each other."

Patrick smiled at the thought of "Brother Bernard," the little church mouse who seemed to love the adventures he was finding in Gubbio. But he also thought of Peter, the "wolf" at St. Anne's.

*Maybe he needed someone to love and take care of him, too, just like Brother Wolf.*

Soon, it was time to say good-bye to their friends in Gubbio. Francis was anxious to head back to Assisi and get working on San Damiano. Patrick remembered the voice coming from the cross, calling them to "repair my church." But how could they possibly do it now? They had no money, no equipment, and no supplies!

Fr. Antonio asked Francis those same questions when he came out to meet them in front of the church.

"We have God's command and Bishop Guido's blessing," Francis assured the poor priest. "God will provide!"

During their first days back at San Damiano, Patrick and Francis collected large stones from the fields surrounding the church.

"Here's an awesome rock!" Patrick would say. Then Francis would come and help dig up the

stone and carry it on his back to the chapel. Bernard also scurried through the fields spotting prime stones and squeaking as he discovered them.

It was hard work, but Francis helped them to pass the time by telling Bible stories or singing songs in French. Patrick felt his arms growing stronger.

"It's so cool to see the building change!"

The work they had begun on one of the walls was almost finished now. Patrick could look at almost every stone and remember where they had found it. It was as if each one had a story to tell.

Soon, there were no more stones to use in the nearby fields.

"We still have three walls to finish!" Patrick said.

But Francis was not worried.

The next day, Patrick and Bernard walked the streets of Assisi with Francis. Francis called out at the top of his lungs:

"Whoever gives me one stone to help rebuild the church at San Damiano will have one reward from the Lord! Whoever gives me two will have two rewards. And whoever gives three will have a triple reward!"

At first Patrick was embarrassed to beg for rocks. But Francis reminded him that San Damiano belonged to all of God's people. "That means they can help us, too!" he said.

Sometimes people would laugh at Francis or even say mean things about him. But if this bothered him, he didn't say so. He would just smile, say a little prayer for the mean person, and move along. Most people, though, were willing to help.

Soon, the little chapel was changing. They built wooden platforms as the walls got taller to help them reach the high places. Every day, San Damiano was looking more and more like a real church!

# ▲ Chapter Fifteen ▲

For days, more and more people from Assisi had been making their way to San Damiano to help with the repairs. Some brought tools and stones. A group of young girls brought cleaning supplies. When one very old woman asked if she could help, Francis had Patrick find her a comfortable place to sit.

"Will you please pray for us as we work?" Francis asked. "That would be a great way to help us repair Christ's church!"

Francis found a job for anyone who came. "This home belongs to all of God's creatures," he

explained. "Christ is present in this place. These brothers and sisters want to be close to Jesus. If we are going to repair the church, we must all help."

Brother Bernard helped, too, clearing the chapel floor of small twigs and pebbles. In fact, Francis involved several of their animal friends. The first time Patrick saw Francis carrying on a conversation with the birds, he thought his friend was crazy. But now, flocks of birds came every day to sing their songs as the builders worked. They were repairing San Damiano, too!

One bright, sunny day, Francis called Patrick over to look at the last wall of the chapel.

"See, Brother Patrick, our work on this wall is almost complete. We will have a special Mass tomorrow with Fr. Antonio inside the chapel."

"Great!" Patrick said. "We can invite all of our friends to celebrate the Eucharist with us."

Patrick remembered back to the first day he'd arrived in Assisi. So much had happened since then. He had even started wearing a long, brown robe with a hood like Brother Francis's over his jeans. But Patrick missed his family and wondered when he would see them again. He thought, *I have so much to tell Katie!*

"I can't believe we've repaired the church!" Patrick said. "We actually did it!"

"But Brother Patrick," Francis smiled, "our repair work is just starting."

Patrick was confused. "This last wall is almost done! Look at this place. It looks great!"

"I have been praying about what Christ said to me from the cross," said Francis. "I believe God is calling us to fix more than just the walls of this one chapel. God needs us to repair his whole Church, to help others find Jesus Christ again by loving and serving each other, especially our poorest brothers and sisters."

"Repair the whole Church?" Patrick thought of St. Anne's and the broken window. And Peter.

"So, to repair the church really means fixing the way we treat people," Patrick said to Francis. "And loving someone, even when they're mean."

Francis smiled. "Maybe the ones who are being mean are the ones who need to be loved most, to help them find true peace in Christ."

The next day, it seemed like every person and animal in Assisi crowded into San Damiano for Mass. Fr. Antonio thanked each one as he welcomed them into the chapel. Brother Francis prayed in the last row with Bernard and his fellow church mice. Patrick, serving at the altar, thought that the little church felt almost like home.

At the Eucharistic Prayer, Fr. Antonio raised up the Host, consecrating the bread into the Body of Christ. Patrick knelt at the side, ringing the altar bells three times as the priest lifted the Host high toward the painted crucifix that hung over the altar.

As he rang the altar bells for the third time, Patrick felt an intense rush of cold wind blow through the doors of San Damiano.

And suddenly, the floor began to rumble, and everything became a blur.

# ▲ Chapter Sixteen ▲

*Clannngggg,* Patrick heard as he knelt on the cold, hard floor. He immediately recognized the sound of St. Anne's ninth noontime Angelus bell. He opened his eyes and saw the broken stained-glass window above him. Next to him was the carved dark stone.

"MCCV! 1205!" he said aloud, suddenly remembering the Roman numerals lesson Mr. Birks had taught their class last month.

He left the vacuum cleaner behind and ran toward the front of the church. His legs were shaking with excitement and exhaustion.

"Katie!" Patrick whispered as he dipped his knee and genuflected in front of the tabernacle. Katie took great care with her cloth and polish to shine every part of the golden locked box that held the consecrated Hosts.

She held a finger to her lips, warning her twin to shush. Then she saw his excited expression and dropped her cloth, pulling him toward the sacristy. The room where Fr. Miguel put on his vestments for Mass was empty.

"Did you hear the bells?" Patrick asked Katie with a huge grin on his face.

"It happened again, didn't it?!" she said.

"I chime traveled to 1205! It was Francis, Katie! I met St. Francis of Assisi!"

She checked the hallway to make sure no one was standing outside the sacristy. "You met the *real* St. Francis?! What was he like? It was Italy, right? Did you eat pizza with him?"

That made Patrick laugh out loud. "Pizza?! Far from it." He thought for a few moments about the big meal he had shared with Francis and Lady Pica his first night in Assisi. Most of their other meals had been whatever scraps kind strangers shared with them.

Patrick spent the next few minutes telling Katie

everything that had happened to him—how he'd met Francis that first day and gone home with him, how they had heard Christ's message from the cross in San Damiano, and how Francis had reacted.

"Go and repair my church…which is falling into ruin?" Katie tried repeating the message back to Patrick. "And so then you went back and fixed up the church? What was it called again, St. Damien's?"

"San Damiano," Patrick corrected her. "At first, I thought we were there to fix up that *one* church. And believe me, it needed fixing. I don't know how Bernard could even live there…"

"Wait," Katie said. "Who's Bernard? Another saint?"

"A mouse," Patrick smiled. "But anyway, I think I was wrong. It wasn't just that one church."

"A *mouse*?" Katie giggled. "Of course you found a new animal friend! But what do you mean, it wasn't just that one church?"

Patrick took Katie by the arm and quietly led her outside to the garden below the broken St. Francis window.

He pointed up to the hole in the stained glass. "Our church is people, right? So, if the Church is broken, maybe it's because some of our people are broken! Maybe there's someone who really needs our help...someone like Peter."

# ▲ Chapter Seventeen ▲

"Wow." Katie looked up at the hole in the window. "I think I see what you mean!"

"I just have this feeling," Patrick said, "that there's some reason this window was broken."

"Yeah, we can fix the window, but maybe that's not really going to fix the problem that's hurting St. Anne's."

"Right! Maybe if we went to Peter and found out what's really wrong, he'd admit to breaking the window."

"But wouldn't he just be in trouble then?"

Patrick remembered the angry wolf in Gubbio. "Maybe, but I bet people would forgive him.

We're a family, right? It's our job to love each other and support each other."

The twins didn't even hear Fr. Miguel walk up behind them.

"Mr. and Miss Brady," he said, "is there some sort of a problem that has you distracted from your Cleaning Team assignments?"

Patrick pointed up to the St. Francis window and said, "We think we may know who has done that!"

The priest looked up at the damage. "We have our security officer reviewing the video from that night, but we can't see the face of the person who threw the brick."

"Father," Katie said, glancing at Patrick, "do you know Peter in our class?"

Fr. Miguel looked again at the damaged window. His mouth turned down at the corners. "I do. I know his family well. I had dinner at their house just last week."

"Father," said Patrick, "we just have this feeling that Peter is hurting, and for some reason, he might have broken this window."

"Kids," said Fr. Miguel, "I honestly don't think it's helpful for us to be accusing people of something as serious as this without knowing for certain what happened. The police are investigating the crime."

"We don't mean to accuse him," Patrick said, "but something's definitely wrong with Peter."

"Yeah!" Katie nodded in agreement. "He's really looking for a fight!"

"He's always been sort of tough," Patrick said, "but lately something seems really messed up. He's mad all the time. And he's definitely big and strong enough to have thrown that brick."

Fr. Miguel listened silently.

"We were thinking," Patrick said, "that we should really reach out to Peter. He seems to be hurting. Maybe if he knows we love him, he'll want to help with the repairs."

"Repairs?" Fr. Miguel gave Patrick a curious look. "You want to *repair* St. Anne's?"

Patrick nodded, thinking again of the wolf. He knew that fixing a window wouldn't really solve the bigger problem. One of their St. Anne's families was hurting and needed help and love. "I thought that all of us kids could work together to find the money to repair the window. And maybe Peter would want to help. Do you think Katie and I could go with you to see Peter later?"

Fr. Miguel smiled up at the image of St. Francis in the broken window. "I think that a visit to Peter and his family would be a great way to start getting this old church repaired."

# ▲ Chapter Eighteen ▲

Dad joined the twins and Fr. Miguel on the visit to Peter's family. The two men chatted in the front seat of the van on the way.

"How is Collette doing?" Dr. Brady asked.

"It's rough," Fr. Miguel answered. "It's been hard on the whole family..."

In the back seat, Katie and Patrick glanced at each other.

"Dad," Patrick asked, "is something wrong with Mrs. Sipe?"

Dad nodded. His voice was low with concern. "Mrs. Sipe has been sick for a few months. She is being treated by a terrific doctor, but it has been a scary time for them."

"Is she going to be OK?" asked Katie.

"We hope so," Fr. Miguel responded, "but her illness is serious."

"Wow," said Patrick. "We really need to pray for the Sipes. Let's find out how else we can help."

Fr. Miguel rang the doorbell. There was ferocious barking from behind the door.

"Quiet down, Leo!" a voice called from inside. "Hey, Max, come get Leo and take him out back!"

As the barking got quieter, the door opened. Peter's dad, Mr. Sipe, stretched his hand out to shake Fr. Miguel's and Dr. Brady's hands. "Hey, Father! Hi, Doc! It's great to see you again. And hello to you two," he said to the kids.

"Thanks for letting us come over, Mr. Sipe," Patrick said. "We were wondering if we could talk to Peter.

"Sure, happy to have you," Mr. Sipe replied. "Why don't you all sit down and make yourselves comfortable."

The twins followed Mr. Sipe into the living room. Peter came out of a bedroom down the hall. "I'll be right back, Mama," he said, holding a tray with a bowl of soup and a glass half filled with water.

"Hi, Peter," Patrick said, his voice shaking a little.

"Hi, Peter," said Katie, feeling shy.

"What are you two doing here?" Peter growled at the twins, suddenly in a bad mood.

"Kids," said Fr. Miguel, "Dr. Brady and I are going to visit Mrs. Sipe for a few minutes." He greeted Peter with a nod.

"I guess I should take you out back," Peter grumbled.

Nervously, Patrick and Katie followed him through the sliding glass door. Peter's massive bulldog, Leo, was sitting on the patio. As they closed the door, he picked up a red plastic ball with his teeth. Then he ran to Patrick and dropped the ball at his feet.

Patrick tossed it to the opposite end of the yard. "We wanted to talk with you, Peter," he said as he watched Leo chase it.

"Why?" Peter asked, looking suspicious.

"How's your Mom doing?" Patrick asked. "I'm sorry…we didn't even know she was sick."

"Um, she's OK," Peter looked down and kicked the grass.

"It must be really hard for you and Max," Patrick said. "I'd be scared if my mom was sick."

Katie nodded in agreement. "And I think it would be hard to help take care of her. I mean, moms are supposed to take care of kids, right?"

Peter blinked and looked away. "I guess."

"But sometimes things don't work out like we want," Patrick said. He thought of Francis's father, and how hard it was on him to see his son choose a different path. "We just want you to know that we're here for you and your family—Katie and me for sure, but really all of St. Anne's."

"So you two think you can come in here and fix everything?" Peter said angrily.

"Peter," Patrick said. "I know it's not the same thing, but when our Mom and Dad were waiting to adopt Hoa Hong, our family went through some hard times."

"We didn't want to tell anyone," Katie said, "but we really should have asked for some prayers. It would have helped to have friends on our side."

"Yeah," continued Patrick, "we just want you to know that we're with you. We're your family."

Peter looked at the ground, and after a long pause, he started to talk.

"Things are really bad right now," the tall boy said. His voice cracked. "My dad's not working, my mom's sick, and it just feels like everything is messed up."

Katie and Patrick waited for him to continue. Peter was silent before finally turning to the twins.

"I was walking Leo over by the church the other night," Peter said, wiping his nose with the back of his hand, "and we stopped in the Mary Garden for him to get a drink in the fountain. I was mad that night. Mad at God, mad at my mom's sickness, mad at everything…"

The twins listened as Peter explained what had happened. When he finished, Patrick made a suggestion.

"Since Fr. Miguel is here, maybe you could spend a few minutes alone talking with him about the window and everything else that's going on."

Peter took a deep breath, trying to calm himself down.

"And then," Patrick continued, "we can all figure out together how we can help your family, and how we can repair St. Anne's."

Fr. Miguel came to the door, and Peter tossed Leo's ball to Patrick.

"Father," Peter said, "can I talk to you for a few minutes?"

Then the toughest kid in Mr. Birks's class wiped a tear from his eye, gave Katie and Patrick each an awkward hug, and followed their pastor back into the house. A few minutes later, Fr. Miguel came and opened the glass door to the yard.

"Why don't you come inside?" the priest invited them.

Katie and Patrick entered the little living room. They saw their dad sitting on the couch next to Mr. Sipe. Peter stood in the corner, looking upset.

"Kids," Fr. Miguel said, "Peter has shared with me what he told you about the window. I thought you'd like to tell him about your idea for getting it repaired."

"Peter, we really want to help you and your family," Patrick said. "We thought of some great ideas for fundraisers. This way, our whole church can get involved in the repairs."

Peter looked at Patrick and Katie with shock. "Wow," he said, "you guys would do that?"

"We're your family," Patrick said. "When one of us is hurting, we've all gotta come together to fix the problem. What do you say? Should we do it?"

Peter stood up, walked across the room, and placed his hand in Patrick's with a smile. "Let's get to work!"

# ▲ Chapter Nineteen ▲

On Monday morning before school, Patrick and Katie went to Sr. Margaret's office to make an announcement on the loudspeaker. After the bell and morning prayers, Sr. Margaret introduced Katie and Patrick. They took turns speaking into the big silver microphone.

"Hey, you guys, it's Patrick."

"And Katie…"

"We need you to help us repair the church," Patrick explained.

"Yeah," said Katie, "we're all going to be raising money to get the St. Francis window fixed."

"Sr. Margaret said we can have a jog-a-thon, and we're going to have a bake sale, too," Patrick said with excitement.

"And we need your ideas!" Katie said. "So, come to a meeting in the Mary Garden today during lunch. We're all going to work together to repair the church!"

From his seat in the back row, Peter smiled for the first time in weeks.

After the lunchtime meeting in the Mary Garden, it seemed like all of St. Anne's was buzzing about how to raise money to repair the window. For the first time, nobody was whispering about who they thought had broken it. Instead, everyone just wanted to be part of fixing it. On the wall at school, Mr. Birks's class hung a poster that looked like a big thermometer. Every time they received a donation or earned money for the repairs, they colored in a part of it.

The jog-a-thon got them off to a great start. Sr. Margaret gave the students permission to bring their pets that morning, since the event was dedicated to fixing the St. Francis window. Kids ran around the dirt track holding leashes with dogs and cats and even a goat and a pot-bellied pig! Peter and Patrick ran side by side with Leo, while Francis the frog hopped along behind them.

The dads in the Knights of Columbus group came up with some fun ways to raise money too. Mr. Daniels donated gelato, a special kind of frozen treat made in Italy, for a sale. All the money they earned went directly to the "Francis Fund," as the twins had started calling it. Everyone pitched in with ideas. They washed cars, did extra chores around their houses, sold old toys and books, and recycled cans, bottles, and newspapers.

Peter and Patrick met after school to mow lawns. Little by little, Peter began to open up.

"I was just so frustrated," he said one day. "I felt like God had left us all alone."

Patrick put his hand on Peter's shoulder. "You are never alone! Sometimes it's hard to understand why bad things happen, but God's love is always with us. And you have lots of friends, too! We're here for you."

Peter shyly fist-bumped his friend. Patrick smiled and imagined what Francis might say. He could picture Brother Bernard wiggling his ears in approval.

Slowly but surely, the thermometer on Mr. Birks's wall started to fill up. "We'll have all the money for the Francis Fund by the end of the week," Katie said to Patrick. "The window is going to look so awesome when it gets repaired!"

"I've been thinking about that," Patrick said. "What if we didn't spend all of the money on the window?"

"But that's why we started the Francis Fund, Patrick," Katie replied. "To fix it!"

"To fix the *church*, right? But maybe we're already doing that. Look how people have come together. We're more like a family than ever. It's like St. Anne's is one big home, and we're all fixing it together!"

"You're right," Katie agreed. "Even Peter, Mr. Sipe, and Max have been helping out with every event."

"Mrs. Sipe is still sick, and his dad is still not back to work," Patrick reminded her. "Maybe we should talk to Fr. Miguel and see if we might be able to use some of the Francis Fund we raised to help Peter and his family."

"I think that's a great idea!" Katie smiled.

# ▲ Chapter Twenty ▲

Finally, the day that everyone at St. Anne's had been working for arrived. For the last week, workers had been on tall ladders fixing the old window. The church was packed full for Sunday Mass. The Knights of Columbus came in with their special suits and fancy hats and swords. Mr. Sarkisian's choir sang beautifully. Patrick and Katie served on the altar. Peter and his family sat in the front row and brought up the gifts of bread and wine at the offertory. The twins were happy to see Mrs. Sipe with them. Peter's mom looked tired and weak, but so happy to be celebrating Mass with her St. Anne's family.

When Mass was over, Fr. Miguel invited everyone to gather in the nave near the back of the church for a good view of the St. Francis window. It had been fully covered while the workmen were doing their repairs. As the twins walked toward the window, Peter joined them.

"Um, Patrick, Katie, can I talk to you for a minute?" the tall boy asked.

"Sure, Peter," Katie said with a smile. "What's up? Are you excited to see the fixed window?"

"Yeah!" Patrick agreed. "It's gonna be awesome!"

Peter stared down at his feet. "I just wanted to say thanks. You guys were pretty cool about all of this. You both helped me to understand that God still loves me and my family, even when bad things happen."

"We're here for you, Peter," Patrick said. "Helping each other in times like this helps all of us understand how much God loves us, even when we mess up!"

"Yeah," Katie joked, "that's a lesson Patrick's definitely learned a time or two!"

They went to stand with their families. Patrick parked himself under the window near the dark stone with the engraved numbers.

"MCCV," he smiled to himself. Working on his St. Francis of Assisi report for school, Patrick had learned that 1205 was the year St. Francis had heard the message of the crucifix at San Damiano. Patrick remembered his time in Assisi. The whisper he'd heard in San Damiano replayed in his mind.

"It's time to unveil the window," Fr. Miguel said, interrupting Patrick's daydream. "But first, I want to share a few words. Some members of our St. Anne's family came to me recently to talk about the Francis Fund."

The priest smiled at Patrick and Katie, standing next to Peter and his family near the dark stone in the wall.

"These friends explained to me that they thought it was important for us to fix this old window. But they also wanted us to use the Francis Fund to help St. Anne's become an even stronger church family. Part of repairing this church is helping our family here grow even closer to Jesus. And we do that by seeing and serving Jesus in each other. And by helping those in need."

Katie gave Patrick a big smile. He playfully stuck his tongue out at her, then gathered her in for a little hug.

"So, Bishop Robert and I have decided to use a portion of the Francis Fund to make a simple repair to this window," Fr. Miguel explained. "And we have used some of the fund to make a donation to a family in our parish who needs some help right now during a challenging time."

The congregation clapped happily at this news.

"The Francis Fund will keep going so that we can help other families in need," Fr. Miguel

continued, "because the work of repairing our church will really never be finished."

With that, he pulled down the large black curtain.

The crowd gasped and started talking excitedly.

The broken spot in the window had been repaired with a simple piece of red glass in the shape of a heart. The sun shone through that spot brilliantly. Patrick's eyes followed the rays of the sun as they lit up the area where Peter stood with his family.

Below the old stone in the wall, a tiny brown creature stood on his back legs. The church mouse looked up at Patrick, wiggled his ears, and then scurried off in search of his next mission.

# ▲ The Real St. Francis of Assisi ▲

Giovanni Francesco Bernardone was born in 1181 at Assisi in Umbria. Francis's father was a successful merchant. He grew up in a comfortable home with fine clothing and plenty to eat. Francis loved to sing and play games. As a young boy, he went to church but was not very religious.

When he was a young man, Francis became a soldier and went away to war. He was injured and held as a prisoner. After the war, Francis was very sick. He began to pray and grew so close to Jesus that he decided to give away all his family's money. He devoted himself to living out what Jesus had taught in the Gospels.

More than anything, Francis wanted to help the poor and to be close to God in prayer. With his words and actions, Francis taught everyone he met to know and love Jesus. Soon, there were many other brothers and sisters who wanted to follow Francis, to live simply like he did and to serve with him. Francis was so humble that he never became a priest, but he gave his whole life to service and prayer.

Francis wrote many special prayers and poems. Legendary stories tell us that St. Francis tamed a wolf around 1220, and he is known for his love for all of God's creatures. St. Francis of Assisi died in 1226, but his lessons live on and continue to teach us how to love one another, to love the world around us and all creation, and to love God with all our hearts. We pray through his intercession as a patron saint of animals, of the environment, and of families.

**The Prayer before the Crucifix at San Damiano**
Most High, glorious God,
enlighten the darkness of my heart
and give me true faith,
certain hope and perfect charity,
sense and knowledge, Lord,
that I may carry out
Your holy and true command.

# ▲ Discussion Questions ▲

1.  The kids at St. Anne's school bring their pets to school for a blessing on the feast day of St. Francis of Assisi. Does your family have a pet? How is your pet a special part of your family?
2.  Fr. Miguel suggests praying for the person who broke the window. Why should we pray for someone who did something bad?
3.  Patrick, Katie, and their friends try to figure out who might have broken the window. Why should we be very careful of accusing someone of doing something wrong without having all the facts?
4.  Patrick and Katie help clean the church to get ready for Bishop Robert's visit. What is the name of your bishop? How is your bishop a spiritual shepherd for your parish?
5.  Francis shares with Patrick that he feels called to help the poor in his community. What are some ways that your family can help those who do not have food or shelter?
6.  Patrick and Francis pray together in the Chapel of San Damiano. Where are some of your favorite quiet places to pray? Why is it important to pray before you make an important decision?
7.  Francis helped the families of Gubbio to make peace with the wolf. How can you make peace with a friend after you've had a disagreement?
8.  Patrick and Bernard joined with many others from Assisi to work on fixing San Damiano. Why is everyone in your parish important to the work that is done to make the church a spiritual home?
9.  Patrick and Katie recognize that Peter is hurting and go out of their way to help his family. What are some ways that you can help a friend who is going through a challenging time?
10. The St. Anne's church family creates the "Francis Fund" to help parish families who are in need. How can your family or parish reach out to help people in your community who are in need of extra love and support?